To Makayla
Fs. Nanny + Poppy
   Mac Neil

Christmas 2011

My Goat Gertrude

Starr Dobson

Illustrated by
Dayle Dodwell

NIMBUS
PUBLISHING

To Nan.

Thanks for the Country House.

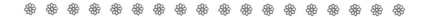

Copyright text © 2011, Starr Dobson
Copyright illustrations © 2011, Dayle Dodwell

Nimbus Publishing Limited
3731 Mackintosh St, Halifax, NS B3K 5A5
(902) 455-4286 nimbus.ca

Printed and bound in China

Cover design: Heather Bryan
Interior design: Jenn Embree
Author photo: Alex MacAulay

Library and Archives Canada Cataloguing in Publication

Dobson, Starr
My goat Gertrude / Starr Dobson ; illustrated by Dayle Dodwell.
ISBN 978-1-55109-861-6

1. Pets—Anecdotes—Juvenile literature. 2. Goats—Juvenile literature. 3. Dobson,
Starr—Childhood and youth—Juvenile literature. I. Dodwell, Dayle II. Title.
SF416.2.D63 2011   j636.088'7   C2011-903919-2

Nimbus Publishing acknowledges the financial support for its publishing
activities from the Government of Canada through the Canada Book Fund
(CBF) and the Canada Council for the Arts, and from the Province of Nova
Scotia through the Department of Communities, Culture and Heritage.

A portion of the proceeds from the sale of this book
will be donated to Special Olympics Nova Scotia.

Welcome to the Country
House. It's our home.
We have plenty of bugs,
mice, and dust bunnies
that live here too, but
we don't mind.

"There's no use fixing up an
old place like this," says Dad.

We all agree. We love
the Country House
just the way it is.

There are five of us here—Mom,
Dad, and three girls: Starr (that's me),
Stacey, and Shannon. We also have a
turtle named Rocky and a big, black
dog called Chips who sticks to me
like glue. And we have Gertrude.

You see, Dad brought us home a surprise
in his truck one day. He told us he had
something big and white that would
help with work around the house. Mom
was sure it would be a clothes dryer.

But it wasn't.

Instead, Dad brought home an
awkward-looking, snow-white
goat. Her stringy little beard
was blowing in the wind as she looked
around with her curious yellow eyes.

Mom was not happy. But the rest of us
sure were.

Right away, the goat started eating
the grass. Dad smiled and said, "See?
She's helping out already."

I named her Gertrude Allawishes
that day, because it just seemed
to fit. Everyone agreed.

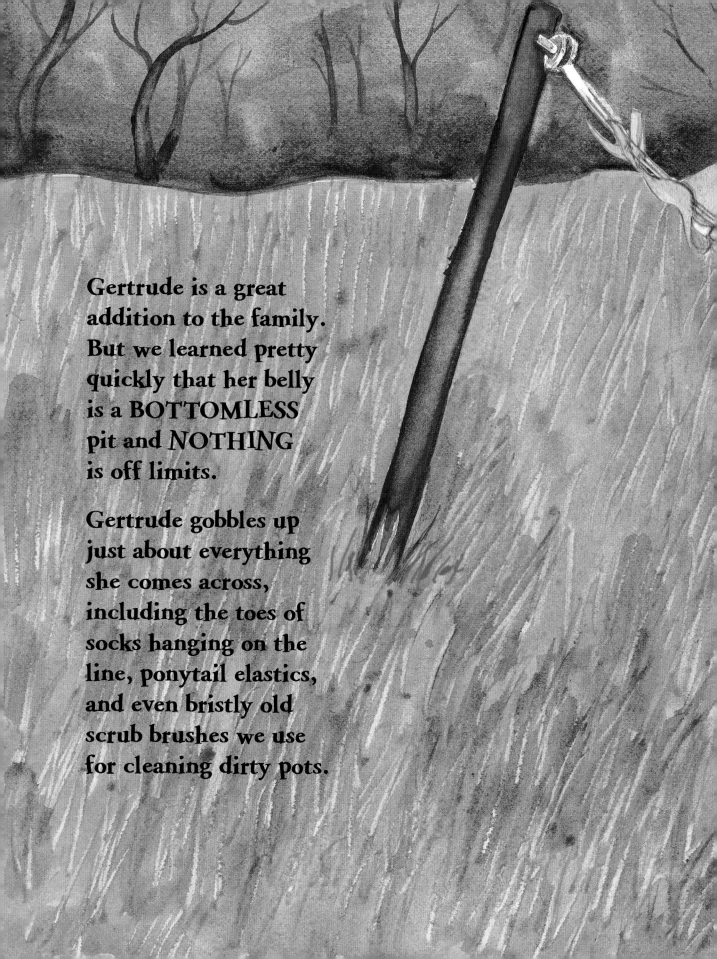

Gertrude is a great
addition to the family.
But we learned pretty
quickly that her belly
is a BOTTOMLESS
pit and NOTHING
is off limits.

Gertrude gobbles up
just about everything
she comes across,
including the toes of
socks hanging on the
line, ponytail elastics,
and even bristly old
scrub brushes we use
for cleaning dirty pots.

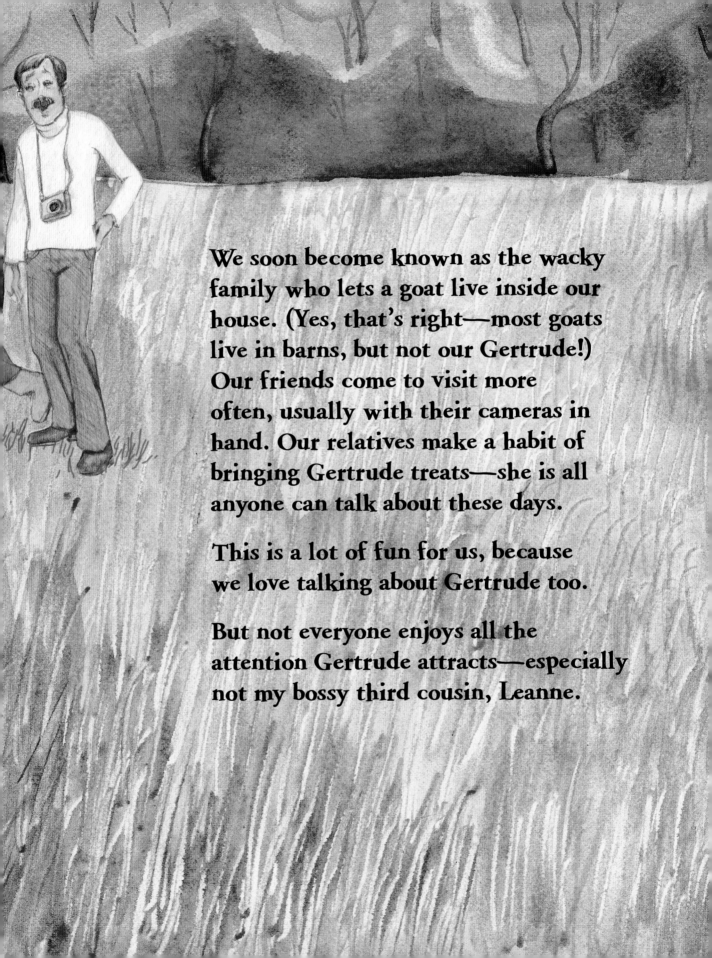

We soon become known as the wacky family who lets a goat live inside our house. (Yes, that's right—most goats live in barns, but not our Gertrude!) Our friends come to visit more often, usually with their cameras in hand. Our relatives make a habit of bringing Gertrude treats—she is all anyone can talk about these days.

This is a lot of fun for us, because we love talking about Gertrude too.

But not everyone enjoys all the attention Gertrude attracts—especially not my bossy third cousin, Leanne.

Leanne is six months
older than me. She thinks
that means she's smarter.
I just think she's more
annoying. I like to have fun
and get dirty. She likes to braid her
hair and paint her nails. She knows
I love candy and usually comes
to visit with two tasty treats.

But one day she shows up with just
one of our favourite chocolate bars.

When I see it, I begin to
anticipate that first bite
of chewy caramel covered
in milk chocolate.

But instead of sharing,
Leanne dangles the bar
in front of my face,
saying, "I've got a Wig
Wag and you don't!"

Now, usually I'd just walk
away, but on this day I
really feel like chocolate.

While she
continues to
tease me, I can't
help but reach
out and try to snatch
the bar from her hand.

It doesn't work. She quickly
hides it behind her back. But
that just makes me want
to eat it even more!

I run around behind her and Chips starts to bark, just like he always does when he thinks I'm in trouble. The next thing I know, Leanne is running away from me, I'm chasing after her, and Chips is hot on our trail. We circle the old tree in the front yard, zigzag around the bushes, and narrowly avoid banging into each other.

I can tell she's starting to get tired, but she just won't stop. That's when I make a bad mistake. I forget to watch where I'm going. I see the stump, but far too late. My feet fly out from under me, and for a second I'm flying. Then I land with a THUD.

Leanne peels open the
top of the chocolate bar
above me. She smiles and
starts to rub her tummy.
"Mmmmmmmmm,"
she says.

Just as she starts to nibble
I yell, "Stop! Put that
down! I want some too."

Leanne laughs and
sticks out her tongue.
Not to take a bite.
Just to be saucy.

I feel a lump starting to form in my throat. I find it hard to swallow and I know the tears aren't far behind.

My knee hurts, I'm mad at my cousin, and on top of all that, I'm not getting any chocolate.

That's when I notice a flash of white.

Within seconds,
Gertrude moves in
and opens wide.

I can't believe my eyes.

She quickly chomps
down on the Wig
Wag without missing
a beat. She eats it
wrapper and all!

Leanne lets out a scream while
Gertrude happily chews away.
The delicious chocolate caramel
bar disappears before we can even
think about trying to get it back.
All that's left is a silly look of
satisfaction on Gertrude's face.

Our parents come running to see what all the fuss is about.

When they hear our story, Leanne gets scolded for being mean. I get in trouble for trying to grab something that wasn't mine. And Gertrude gets told she's a very bad goat.

Leanne and I sneak peeks at each other and then start to giggle. After all, it was kind of funny to see Gertrude eat a whole candy bar.

Leanne promises to take me a treat of my own next time. I suggest something other than a Wig Wag just in case Gertrude's around. She agrees, gives me a hug, and heads home.

That night after Mom tucks me
into bed, I say goodnight to my
two best friends…Chips and Gertrude.

As they snuggle together on my bedroom floor,
I can't fight the urge to get a bit closer to my
goat. "Gertrude, come on up!" I say.

My heroic goat swiftly jumps onto my
bed almost as quickly as she gulped
down Leanne's chocolate bar. I
give her a squeeze and whisper
"thank you" in her ear.

She nuzzles me back and
gets ready for a special
night's sleep beside
me on my bed.

I drift off thinking that even
though Gertrude shouldn't
have gobbled up Leanne's
chocolate, she did it for ME.

I am so lucky.

I have everything I need
here at the Country House,
including the funniest,
most protective goat
ever, who likes to cuddle
and thinks I'm worth
eating wrappers for!

(Oh, and by the way, my mother did
end up getting my father's goat—
she went to town and bought a big,
white clothes dryer, to really help
with work around the house!)